Jeannine Atkins

Robin's Home

Pictures by
Candace Whitman

Farrar, Straus and Giroux

New York

For the Zimmerman family:
Aaron, Hannah, Samantha, Eliana, George,
and my friend Robyn
—J.A.

For Charles Ethan
—C.W.

Text copyright © 2001 by Jeannine Atkins
Illustrations copyright © 2001 by Candace Whitman
All rights reserved. Distributed in Canada by Douglas & McIntyre Ltd.
Printed and bound in the United States of America by Worzalla
Color separations by Hong Kong Scanner Arts. Typography by Filomena Tuosto
First edition, 2001
1 3 5 7 9 10 8 6 4 2

Library of Congress Cataloging-in-Publication Data

Atkins, Jeannine, date.
    Robin's home / Jeannine Atkins ; pictures by Candace Whitman.— 1st ed.
        p. cm.
    Summary: Robin learns how to fly and build a nest. Includes information on the life
cycle of robins.
    ISBN 0-374-36337-4
    1. Robins—Juvenile fiction. [1. Robins—Fiction.] I. Whitman, Candace, date, ill. II. Title.
PZ10.3.A8756 Ro 2001
[E]–dc21
                                                                          99-86853

Life was good for Robin. He liked
to watch his sister and brother fly.

Whenever he was hungry, his mother
or father brought food.

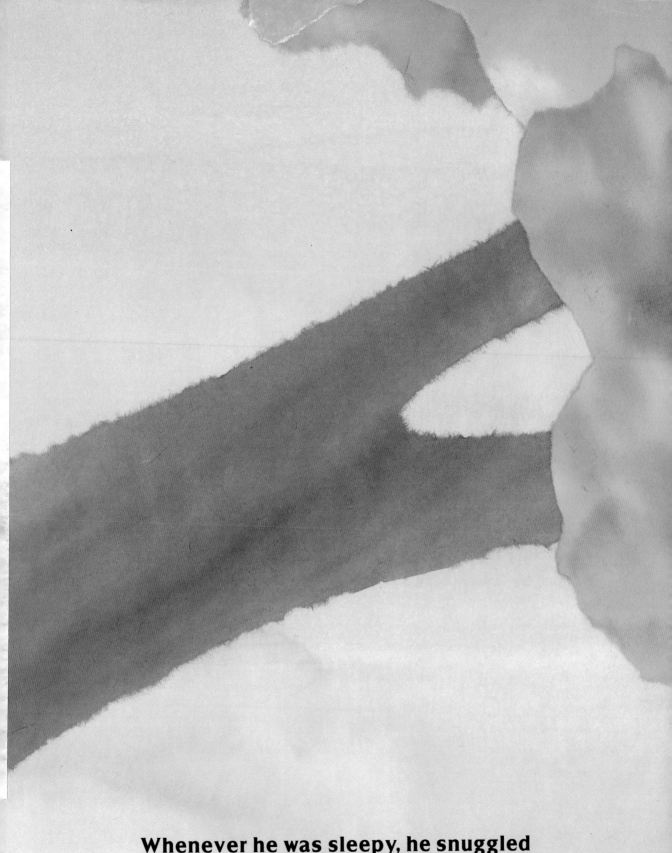

**Whenever he was sleepy, he snuggled
in the nest that fit as perfectly as a hug.**

When he wanted a story, he said,
"Mama, Papa, tell me again about
how you made our nest."

"Your mother found the perfect spot
near a lawn full of food," Papa said.
"We gathered grass and moss for
days," Mama said.

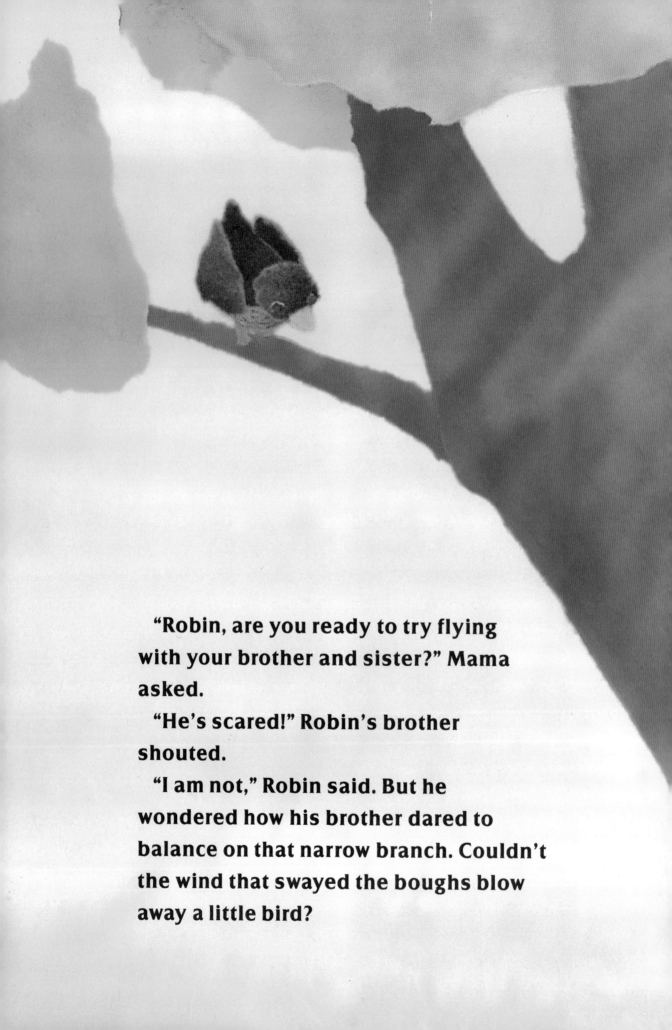

"Robin, are you ready to try flying with your brother and sister?" Mama asked.

"He's scared!" Robin's brother shouted.

"I am not," Robin said. But he wondered how his brother dared to balance on that narrow branch. Couldn't the wind that swayed the boughs blow away a little bird?

Robin snuggled deeper into the nest and said, "Tell me more about how you made our nest."

"Your father found yarn that some children hung for us. They cut it to just the right size," Mama said.

Robin's sister called, "Aren't you ever coming, Robin? The grass tickles my face. The mud cools my feet."

But Robin liked having his feet tucked beneath him, so that he knew exactly where they were. He liked watching the clouds or trying to find the yarn woven among dried grass. He liked to dream with his head resting on the rim of the nest. Why should he leave a home that fit like a hug?

"This is the best nest in the world,"
Robin said. "How did you make it?"
he asked Mama and Papa.

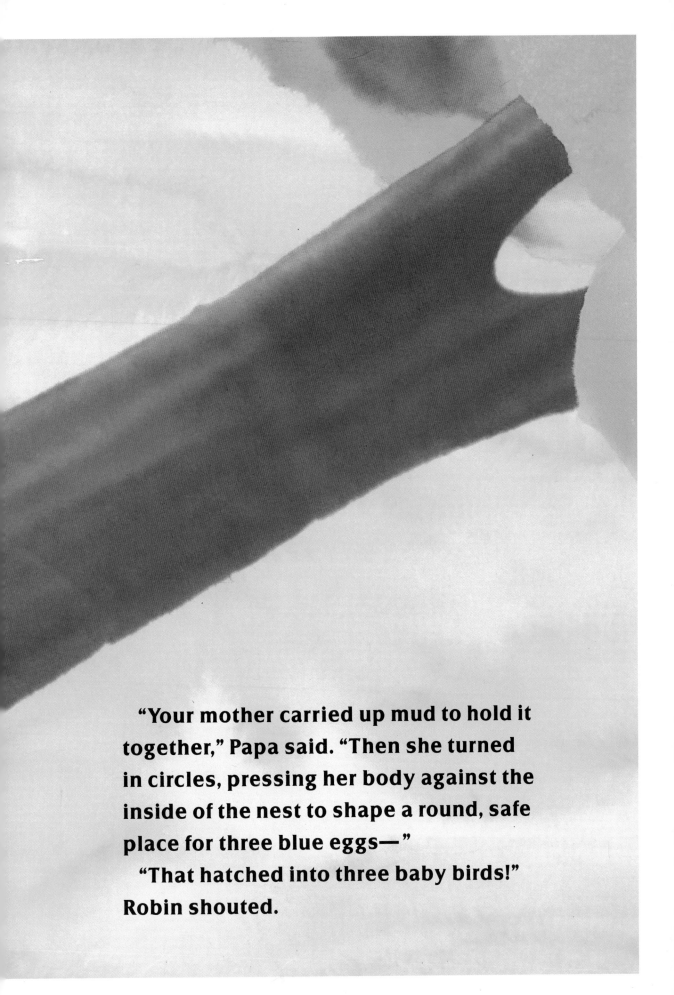

"Your mother carried up mud to hold it together," Papa said. "Then she turned in circles, pressing her body against the inside of the nest to shape a round, safe place for three blue eggs—"

"That hatched into three baby birds!" Robin shouted.

"Someday you will help build a nest," Mama told Robin.

"What if I can't make a nest?" Robin asked.

"You'll find grasses and mud just the way we did," Mama said.

"What if I'm the first bird who can't fly?"

"Every robin can fly," Papa said.

"Really?" Robin felt hopeful.

Robin hopped onto the rim of the nest.
The ground looked awfully far away.

"We'll be right behind you," Mama
said.

"I'll show you where we found the mud
that holds the nest together," Papa said.
"Maybe we'll see the children who hung
the yarn."

Robin spread his wings and leapt.
"Up! Up!" he told himself.

But he was going down. "Oh, no!"
He didn't want to blow away or crash.

Robin flapped his wings harder. He
kept on going down, but in a slow,
zigzagging sort of way.

"Look at me, Papa!" Robin called.
"Mama, I'm in the sky!"

He landed softly.

Then Robin hopped back up into the air.
"Chee! Chee! Cheerilee!" He was flying!

Robin didn't go high. He didn't go fast.
But every day he would go higher and
faster. Now the whole sky was home.

More About Robins

All across North America, robins build nests in the spring and early summer. They like being near lawns, since a lawn is a good place to find worms.

Robins spend days bringing grass and almost anything that's soft and flexible to their nest site. Sometimes people hang yarn or string on trees for robins to weave into their nests. The string should be less than ten inches long so that the birds don't get tangled in it.

People also help by making muddy spots if there hasn't been much rain. The mother robin carries the mud, bit by bit, to the nest. She tamps down the mud with her feet, then presses the grass and mud with her breast to shape the nest. She lines the cup of the nest with fine grasses.

The mother robin lays three to five blue eggs. These must be kept warm and safe, so for the next two weeks the mother rarely leaves the nest. Once the eggs hatch, both the robin mother and father look for worms and insects. They take these to their hungry babies.

The babies quickly get bigger and grow speckled feathers on their breasts. The feathers help them blend in with the trees and ground, protecting them from predators.

Baby robins leave the nest when they're about two weeks old. At first they don't fly far. Often they hop across lawns, tilting their heads to look with one sharp eye for worms. By autumn, the baby robins have red breasts. Now they can fly long distances in search of a warm place to spend the winter. In the spring, they fly back and start families of their own.